The Prince of the Rabbits

WRITTEN BY FELIX MEROUX

ILLUSTRATED BY COOPER EDENS

STAR & ELEPHANT BOOK

THE GREEN TIGER PRESS • LA JOLLA AND LONDON

Text copyright © 1984 by Felix Meroux
Illustrations copyright © 1984 by Cooper Edens
The Green Tiger Press • La Jolla • California 92038
First Edition • First Printing

Library of Congress Catalog Card Number 84-81640
ISBN 0-88138-030-X

For the Wendel family, Tune, and Rice

The prince of the rabbits
was tired of this world.
The grass was always green,
the water always blue.

The prince of the rabbits had seen everything, and he was bored.

He wanted to travel
to another planet. In fact,
he secretly thought
that he was from another world
and was in this one by mistake.

He had many plans
for getting to another planet.
One week he stood on his bed
night after night, waiting
for someone to fly him away.

But it never happened.

Another time he put rocks
with special rings around them
beneath his pillow
and wished that he would awaken
in a different world.

But, when morning arrived,
his toys stared at him
from the shelf
with the same pensive expression
in their eyes, and all the familiar
smells and sounds
were rising from the corridors.

The situation was becoming more
and more desperate. Then, one
night, he awakened to dimly hear
the language of chairs, and
the song two lamps were singing.

In the moonlight every object possessed a voice. There were as many shadows as things, and even they were speaking. The room itself was alive.

The prince began to feel odd,
for he heard his name,
again and again.
And the moon seemed now
to be glaring into the room.
In this light he heard
how the heart of every object
was saddened by his neglect.

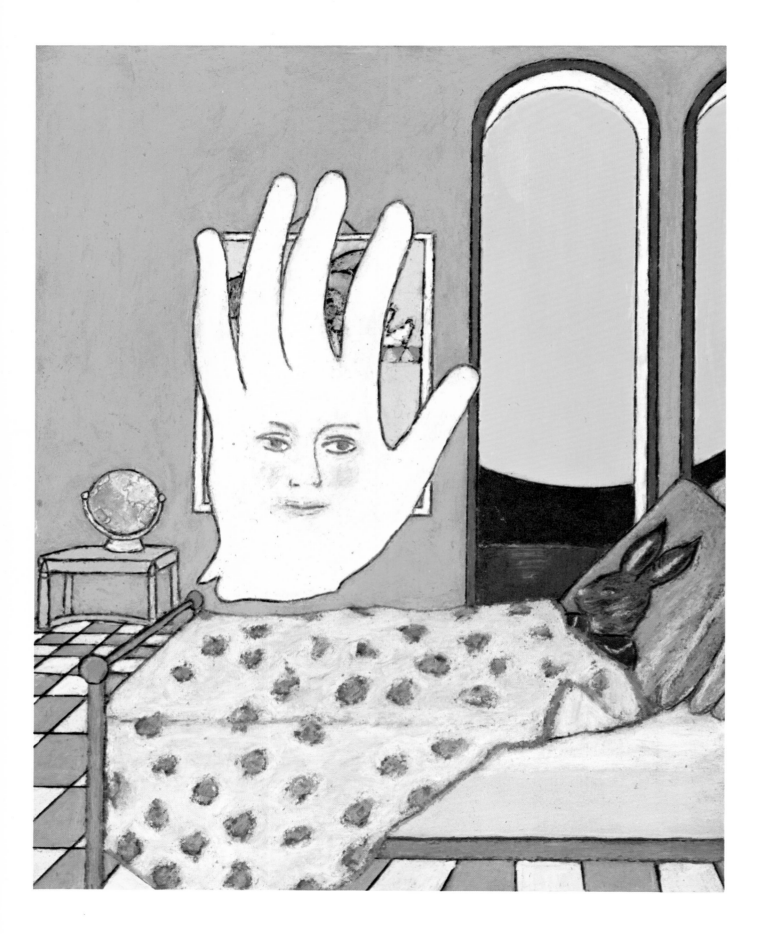

Suddenly, an elegant glove
he had carelessly thrown
to the floor
grew to immense proportions
and loomed
over the side of his bed.

"This world is much more
mysterious than you thought,
little rabbit," it said.

Strangely enough,
this made the prince laugh.

And he laughed

and laughed

and laughed

until two beautiful tears
fell from his eyes.

The Cover Type is Auriol Condensed set by Solotype of Oakland, CA
The Text is Auriol set by Ad/Grafic of Santa Ana, CA
Color separations by Photolitho AG,
Gossau-Zurich, Switzerland.
Printed at Green Tiger Press,
San Diego, California,
USA